Dancin' in the Kitchen

by Wendy Gelsanliter & Frank Christian

illustrated by Marjorie Priceman

G. P. Putnam's Sons ▪ New York

G. P. Putnam's Sons, Reg. U.S. Pat. & Tm. Off. Published simultaneously in Canada
Printed in Hong Kong by South China Printing Co. (1998) Ltd.
Book design by Gunta Alexander. Text set in Lucida Casual
Library of Congress Cataloging-in-Publication Data
Gelsanliter; Wendy. Dancin' in the Kitchen / Wendy Gelsanliter; Frank Christian;
illustrated by Marjorie Priceman. p. cm.
[1. Cookery — Fiction 2. Family life — Fiction 3. Stories in rhyme]
I.Gelsanliter, Wendy II. Priceman, Marjorie (ill.) III. Title PZ8.3.C4567Dan
1998[E]--dc20   95-51099 CIP   AC   ISBN 0-399-23035-1
3 5 7 9 10 8 6 4

For Jessica,
who could dance in the kitchen
all night. —F.C.

To John —W. G.

For Jean —M. P.

It's six o'clock at Grandma's house
We all know that it's time
To step into the kitchen
All in a line.

Grandma turns the music up
We're ready to roll
She hands out the spoons
She hands out the bowls.

We're making chicken and dumplings
The dumplings sit on top.
Did Grandpa add the carrots?
No? Then chop, chop, chop.

Mama snaps the beans
Throws them in the pot
Adds a little water
Steams them 'til they're hot.

Papa takes the beans
Gives them all a butter pat

Puts them on the top shelf
To keep them from the cat.

Dancin' in the kitchen
The family's packed in tight
I think we may be
Dancin' in the kitchen all night.

Brother takes the shortcake
And slips it on a dish

Sis piles up the strawberries   Any way we wish.

I put on lots of whipped cream
I'm no fool
I put it in the fridge
To keep it really cool.

Dancin' in the kitchen
Everyone's a chef
But if the baby gets the shortcake
Then there won't be any left!

Now dinner's ready
And it's time to eat

But the music on the radio
Keeps us dancin' on our feet.

Everybody's hungry
But dinner's got to wait
'Cause all the legs are moving
'Cept the chicken's on the plate.

Grandma sits us down
While the food's still steamin' hot
Grandpa's at the bottom
Grandma's at the top.

Soon dinner's over
And the hour's gettin' late
But I'm dancin' to the kitchen
With nothin' on my plate!

Grandpa does the washin'
We all pitch in to dry
We're still dancin' in the kitchen
With the radio way up high.